Keicia Lyons

Wonderfully Made

Wendy

and the Powerhouse Prayer Group

ISBN NO. 978-1-953760-22-7

Printed in the United States of America

Table of Contents

CHAPTER 1

4th Grade will rock!!!

"*Yes, JESUS loves me, Yes, JESUS loves me,*" The sweet melody of the peaceful song floats throughout the house. Musical notes bounce across the pastel pink comforter, the putrid walls with white trim, and the multi-colored bean bags in the corner with dolls and teddy bears spilling over them like ants on a mountainous hill.

Although the music was beautiful and peaceful to get a morning started, it wasn't what Wendy wanted to hear. "Ugh," she yelled as she covered her ears, "Doesn't my mom know that this song is so 1st grade?" The melodic sounds of the music created a serene feeling in the bedroom, just like her mom liked for her to feel to start a day, but serene was the exact opposite of what Wendy wanted to hear. She tossed and turned in the bed while the music played, then she finally reached for her earbuds to drown out the noise. Wendy hated to feel this way because she knew her mother meant well, but baby music just offended her to her core since she turned nine, and it simply WAS NOT acceptable on the first day of school. "I asked her to treat me like a 4th grader," she said to herself as she sat straight up in the bed and sighed. She continued by saying, "I let it slide for 2nd and 3rd grade, but I'm in 4th grade now, and this is simply NOT ACCEPTABLE,!" and at that very moment, she flung the covers back with a determined mind to prove to her mom that she was just too old for "baby stuff."

She jumped out of the bed and glanced at her vision in the full-body mirror that was hanging on the wall. She needed to know if she looked like a 4th grader, or if her body still screamed "3rd grade."

Wendy stood on her tippy toes. "I'm getting taller, I can feel it," she said, as she looked at her 3'11, 75-pound frame with admiration. She took off her silk bonnet to look at her long, twisted pigtails and pulled them up into one big ponytail on the top of her head.

"I simply cannot look like a little girl," she said, as she twisted her body to view herself from different angles.

She evaluated whether she looked any different, then concluded that she did not.

"Nope," she said, "I haven't changed much, but I still am, and will always be a powerhouse" and with that, she said "Alexa, my fave."

Immediately, Jesus loves me is replaced with a familiar beat, and then the lyrics...

"Ain't nobody stopping my shine, they try to break me, try to take me, but I got Jesus on my side."

"Won't he do it," by Koryn Hawthorne was Wendy's favorite song. It got her pumped in the morning, and that's exactly how she wanted to feel today, her very first day in 4th grade.

"This year, we change classes, and can join the chorus, and can be a fire marshal, and I'm ready," she said, as she stepped into her bathroom which was also a gorgeous pink that coordinated perfectly with her bedroom.

"This year is my year." Wendy thought to herself as she entered the shower while reading her encouraging messages of affirmation that were hanging on the wall. Her mom started a tradition when Wendy entered preschool. She would find encouraging pictures and words every year to make Wendy excited and pumped about the great things that she would experience that year. Their back-to-school shopping would not be for clothes and shoes only. Wendy's mother loved to find anything that would make her children feel encouraged and empowered. They would spend hours on end searching for books and affirming artwork that would inspire and motivate Wendy to be the greatest, most awesome student that she could be.

"I can do all things through Christ who strengthens me." She kept saying as she showered, got dressed, and fixed her hair.

"Mom wants to help me, but I'm too big for that." she thought as she applied her lotion, her lip gloss and then put her pink backpack on her back. "I'm ready to tackle the day," she yelled loudly, as she headed out her bedroom door with a walk so confident that she could move mountains. Wendy quickly turned her lights off, commanded Alexa to stop playing, and went downstairs to join her family for breakfast.

CHAPTER 2

A Breakfast for Winners

Breakfast on the first day of school was always so much fun at Wendy's house. Her mom's family tradition would be to fix a delicious meal of homemade blueberry muffins with melted butter on top, blueberry yogurt, and almond milk to drink. "Breakfast is the most important meal of the day." she would say with a smile while she poured their milk and planted warm kisses on their cheeks. Wendy's mother was a wonderful cook, and she took great pride in making her babies delicious and nutritious meals from scratch, using her bare hands and her mother's secret recipes that were "magnifico," as her dad would say.

As mom swept by while passing out muffins and milk and singing her favorite song "Yes, JESUS loves me", Wendy could smell the delicate scent of her intoxicating skin oil. She loved it so much, and she would sneak and rub it on her neck and hands some mornings to try to smell just like her mom. Wendy loved her mom with all her heart, and she definitely wanted to be like her when she grew up. All of her friends thought that she was amazing, too. She consistently made it her business to go above and beyond to make sure that her kids were happy and healthy, but it never stopped there. She was kind and caring to all of the kids in the neighborhood and at school, and that's why they were constantly having parties and sleepovers at their house. Today, they were focused on what was most important, though. Wendy's parents valued education very much, and they wanted both of their children to have everything that they needed to be their absolute best, so that meant that they had to have a nice hot breakfast and great conversation to get the day started right.

"How's my little 4th grader?" her dad asked as he extended his arms toward Wendy to give her their usual bear hug.

"Not little 4th grader daddy, remember, I'm 9 years old now."

"I know, I know," he said. "I guess my baby's growing up." Just remember

Wendy already knew what he was going to say, so she joined him as they sang in unison

"You'll be my little nugget until you're 101 years old"

Wendy and her dad laughed as they rushed toward their favorite seats and started their usual "first day of school conversations."

"So what types of activities do you guys want to be involved in this year?" Mom asked as she finally got a chance to sit down with her family.

"I want to do football and baseball, and boy scouts, yeah!!!" Walter, Wendy's 6- year -old brother yelled with excitement.

"Whoa, that's a lot, son." dad said, do you think you're ready for all of that?

"I know I am," said Walter, holding up his arms to show his dad his muscles to prove how strong he was.

Everyone else at the table laughed and touched Walter's muscles. They gave him high-fives and simply enjoyed his innocence and exuberance.

"What about you, baby girl?" dad asked, "What are your plans for the year?"

"You know, I've got my powerhouse crew, dad," she said matter- of -factly as if he asked a dumb question and already knew the answer. Her dad looked at her with pride. He admired the young lady that Wendy was blossoming into. She stood on GODLY principles and Biblical truths, and that's exactly how he and his wife had tried to raise both of their children.

"I know you'll be a great leader of the Powerhouse group, baby," her dad said as he started to rise from the table. He walked over to Wendy and planted a kiss on her forehead. "Watch out world, my daughter is on the way," he said, then he gave his son an even bigger high-five and their special handshake, then told him "don't hurt'em, my main man."

"I'll try," Walter said with laughter, as he watched his dad kiss their mom, then head out the door to work.

When dad left, mom said, "OK guys, give me about 30 minutes, and I'll be ready to go."

"Can't we go now?" Wendy said.

"Yeah!!" Walter echoed while he jumped up and down with his hands in the air.

"Hold on you two," their mom said while laughing. She was glad that they were anxious, but she was also trying to calm their excitement just a little. "Let me finish my final touches, ok." She continued by saying I spent my morning making sure that you guys had a nice breakfast, now I need my little munchkins to give me just a minute so we can all walk out looking like a beautiful, well-put-together family." She then said, "Now you guys sit down and watch some TBN kids while I get dressed. Do not get dirty, ok." She coaxed her children in her sweet voice while looking directly at Walter. "OK," he said with a devilish smile. Mom knew that Walter loved his hot wheels, but she also knew that his appearance was important to him too, so she trusted that he would sit down until she could finish preparing herself for the day.

Walter gave her a reassuring look, and with that, she kissed them both and made her way back upstairs.

She came back down in about 25 minutes. Wendy knew how long it was because she had counted every single one of those minutes, and she became more and more excited as each one passed. When her mom finally stepped into the room, Wendy thought she looked like a goddess. Her mother, Lisa, wore her hair in a very neat halo braid this morning. Her earth tone skirt and burgundy blouse looked so beautiful against her caramel skin. Lisa loved to wear wood jewelry and any other type of accessories that emphasized her African descent. She looked beautiful with her pearly white teeth and sparkly eyes, and Wendy and Walter were proud to call her mom.

"Let's go take this world by storm," she said, as she grabbed Walter's hand, and the three of them made their way to the car to start their very exciting day.

CHAPTER 3

Conversations with mom

"So, are you excited, Pumpkin?" her mother asked as they made their way to Brown Academic and Stem Academy. This was the conversation they had every first day of school, but today had to be different. She would no longer be referred to as "Pumpkin" in front of her friends, so she said "Wendy, mom."

"Of course, Wendy" her mom chuckled as she corrected herself.

"It's not funny, mommy," she said as she made a mental note to keep calling her mom, not mommy, "I really need to be respected if I'm going to be the leader of The Powerhouse Crew."

"I know baby", her mom said, just remember, "You'll always be my Pumpkin, even if it's behind closed doors." Those words made Wendy happy, so they both smiled as they thought about what she said.

Wendy understood, so she reached over and kissed her mom. She had a wonderful relationship with both of her parents. Her mother, Lisa Madison, was the librarian at Wendy's school. She was a beautiful brown lady with shoulder-length locks and a style that all of Wendy's friends admired. She usually wore African prints, and she always had a way of wrapping her scarves so neatly around her head or decorating her home or the library so beautifully that people always wanted to be where she was. She attracted peace, and that's what Wendy and her friends loved about her.

"It's your year," her mom said, as Wendy thought to herself "it's always my year, mom."

Confidence had never been a problem for Wendy. Even though her weight was a little bit more than what most people thought was "normal," she was beautiful, and she knew it.

"When has it ever not been my year," she said as she reminded her "didn't I make 2nd place in Science Fair last year, and don't I always make A's & B's"? She said as she leaned down and turned her face up so she was looking into her mother's eyes. They had such a great bond, and Wendy loved every minute of it.

Her relationship with her dad and brother was equally awesome. James Madison was the meteorologist at the local

TV station, and he and Lisa were the parents to two "Wonderfully made kids," Wendy, and 6-year-old Walter.

Lisa and James believed in being excellent in everything that they did. They had both gone to high school and college together, and they loved talking about the fun times they had at their little country college called Fort Valley State University.

"Girl, you haven't lived until you've been to an HBCU homecoming," Lisa would say when she talked to her kids about college. Some of Wendy and Walter's favorite memories were of going down to the farmland of Georgia to THE Fort Valley State University, where their parents went to college, to enjoy homecoming. They loved seeing the drumline and majorettes of the marching bands high step as they danced to the jazziest beats. They also loved eating the food from the vendors on the streets while watching their parents hang out and be silly with their old college friends.

Both sets of their grandparents lived in Georgia. Wendy understood why her mom could cook so well, because her grandmothers could, as her dad would say, "Tear a kitchen up." Whenever they went to visit them, one grandmother cooked fried chicken and potato salad, and the other one made peach cobbler, pound cake, and sweet tea, and when they did this, Wendy and Walter thought they were in heaven. She loved visiting the southern charm of Georgia, and she hoped to possibly live there when she became an adult. Wendy's parents had moved to Indiana when her daddy got a job at the

TV station before Wendy was born. Their family traditions were set up so that Wendy's parents would usually visit Georgia for Thanksgiving, and both sets of grandparents would come to Indiana to visit them for Christmas.

Walter was quiet in the back seat of their white 2018 Mercedes Benz GLE class SUV.

"And how are you doing, my little king?" Lisa asked her son as she inquired about his feelings since they were finally on their way to school.

"Mom, I got this," her little man said. Lisa loved the fact that her children were confident. She taught them to be kind and loving, but she and James also reminded them that they were royalty and that they could "Do all things through CHRIST who gave them strength to do it.

After she parked the car, and everybody got out, Lisa grabbed the hands of both of her children, and they knew what that meant. All three of them automatically bowed their heads as she began to pray over her kids and the new school year.

"Dear HEAVENLY FATHER," she said. "You have allowed us, your children, to begin a new school year, LORD." The birds chirping in the background, and the sounds of pebbles dropping in the pond behind the school made the prayer sound so beautiful as Lisa poured her heart out to THE LORD. She continued by saying, "We know that it is simply because of your love and your favor that we are here, but we thank you LORD, and we appreciate your grace and your mercy."

Wendy and Walter stood very still and listened attentively as their mother recited her prayers. The school that they attended was a CHRISTIAN school, so most of the parents started the first day with prayer. This was a ritual for Lisa and her family, and she intended to do it until both of her children graduated from high school.

"I pray that you see fit to open my children's hearts and minds to receive the knowledge that you want to give them LORD," she said. "Please help them to be eager students, and to soak up all of the knowledge that they can get, so they can be better servants to you, LORD. Please let them be good stewards of your word in their classrooms, and allow their classmates and teachers to see your light through them."

Lisa could feel the HOLY SPIRIT moving as she spoke.

"And LORD," she said, "Please keep these hallways and classrooms safe from hurt, harm, and danger. We know that this earth is a horrible and dangerous place, but we are believing that we are safe with you LORD. So in the name of your precious son, we pray for these blessings, and we receive them in his name, Amen."

Wendy and Walter repeated "amen," then they all embraced for a group hug. After that, Wendy walked toward her classroom while Lisa and Walter walked holding hands and headed toward his classroom. "It's going to be a great day, I can feel it," Wendy just kept saying to herself as she beamed her confident smile and spoke to everyone she came across.

CHAPTER 4

Mrs. Jordan's class

When she finally got to her classroom, she was so happy to see her teacher. Wendy loved her teacher, Mrs. Jordan. Mrs. Jordan was about 34 or 35 years old, and she was a person who obviously loved her job very much. All of her last year students talked about how awesome her class incentives were. She would allow her students to get free time on Fridays if they got their work done, and she took pride in never raising her voice when she got angry. She always wore the latest fashions, and she thought that people didn't know it, but she would sometimes buy clothes and even groceries for some of the less fortunate students in her classroom. All of these things were great reasons to love Mrs. Jordan, but

Wendy's main reason for loving her was because she reminded her of her mom. She was such a beautiful lady, and she always smelled nice, just like Lisa. Wendy couldn't wait to get into her classroom. Last year, Mrs. Jordan's class had such fun activities, and she gave them the best parties. Her subject was ELA, but she always treated her homeroom class the best. Her classroom was decorated with beautiful streamers and kites. She had a special reading corner with a gorgeous frilly rug and a painted bookshelf with all of the greatest books.

Wendy had known Mrs. Jordan her whole life because she was one of her mom's best friends and sorority sisters. Almost everybody in the school lived in the small town of Canvas, Indiana, and most of them had known each other their entire lives. Wendy was excited to see her best friends Alexis, Paula, and Tim. They had all been best friends since kindergarten, and they made up the Powerhouse Prayer group, better known as the PPG. Wendy's mom taught her the power of prayer when she was a little girl, and she shared this knowledge with her best friends. Together, they had prayed themselves through having a mean teacher, science fair scares, and the fear of having a pet snake as a class pet. The Powerhouse Prayer Group was ready to take on the obstacles of the new school year, so they came fully equipped with the full armor of GOD.

"Alright class, find your seats." Mrs. Jordan said as they made their way to their desks. After everyone was seated, she started calling roll.

"Jasmine," she said and Jasmine raised her hand and said "Here."

"Michael," she said, and the most mischievous boy since kindergarten jumped up very quickly to make everybody laugh and said "Present," then he put his hand up to his head to salute Mrs. Jordan like he was a soldier. Everybody laughed.

As Mrs. Jordan continued to call all of the names in the class, Wendy and her friends exchanged hi-fives and hugs to say that the gang was back together, and ready to have a great year.

Everybody was in a good mood and was laughing and talking except one boy. He was a strange little boy who sat in the back of the room. He wasn't the only new kid in the class. There were two new girls and another boy, but he was the only one that didn't talk, and, for some reason, that bothered Wendy.

So, when she and her Powerhouse group got together that day in their free time, Wendy called an emergency meeting.

"PPG, come to order," she said, as her friends gathered around.

"What's going on?" asked Paula.

Paula was one of Wendy's best friends, and she was the secretary of The PPG.

"There's a boy in our class who's sitting all alone," Wendy said, "and we need to make him feel welcomed."

"Uh-oh," said Jasmine, "The worrier who wasn't really a part of the group, but a tag-a-long sometimes said, "sounds like a code 88854, and they all said together "no one in the classroom will ever feel lonely."

"That's right," Wendy said, "so what are we going to do about it?"

"Let's all go talk to him when we get back inside." Paula said matter of factly, as if to say "it's so simple."

"That sounds good," said Wendy, but what if he doesn't talk?

"Well, we'll just make him talk," said Tim, the only boy in the group who always tried to throw his weight around, even though he was the shortest and smallest kid in 4th grade, and most people called him shrimp.

"Let's be careful guys," Wendy said, "we want him to feel welcomed, not bullied."

"We won't be obvious, said Paula, we'll just act like we just happened to look his way, how does that sound?"

"Yeah, that sounds good." Alexis, Wendy's best friend, said as she nodded her head in agreement.

They all thought about it and concluded that this method was best. The group put their final touches on the idea just as

Mrs. Jordan appeared in the doorway to indicate that it was time to go back inside. Each member was giggling with excitement because they just knew that today they would make somebody happy, and that was the whole purpose of The PPG.

"We got this." Wendy said, as they put their hands together in a circle and yelled "PPG, may JESUS be seen in me," then they ran toward Mrs. Jordan, excited about what they were planning to do.

CHAPTER 5

10 good things about you

The PPG headed back into the classroom with excitement on their lips, ready to save the day. They already knew that Mrs. Jordan had something fun planned for them to do, and they couldn't wait to include Terrance in the excitement.

Mrs. Jordan was known throughout the school for being a fun teacher. Everybody always wanted to be in her class because they knew that great things were just waiting to happen. When all of the students were in and settled, she introduced them to a game called "classmate charades."

"All of you are going to pull a classmate's name out of this hat," she said, "but do not say who you have." "Don't even open the paper," she emphasized. "Choose your name, then wait for further instructions."

Mrs. Jordan knew that some people would try to open the paper anyway, especially devilish Corey, so she watched them very closely. When every student had a name, she said, "Now, I want each of you to think of ten positive qualities about the classmate you have chosen. Most of you have known each other since kindergarten, so you can come up with nice things to say. You can talk about their looks, or how they dress, but that's pretty basic. This is meant to be a fun, bonding activity, so let's make it that way. Talk about what you know their hobbies are. Talk about their talents, their favorite subjects, their pets, and their parents, whatever. I just want you to think of 10 positive things to say about your classmates. Do not tell anyone who you have. I'm giving you 15 minutes to do this, then we will move on to the next portion of the activity. If you have a new student, or you cannot think of 10 things, talk about their beautiful appearance or name as many things as you can. Now, open your papers."

Wendy couldn't wait to open hers, and when she saw the name she had, she couldn't believe her luck. On her paper read the name, Terrance.

"Yes," she thought to herself, "This is it." "This is the perfect opportunity to make him feel special and welcomed in this classroom." Her mind started racing because she knew that this was her chance to make magic happen.

Wendy thought very deeply about her list. "Please GOD, help me to say the right things" she prayed to herself. Wendy's mother had taught her to always pray when she didn't know what to do. She had been raised to depend on GOD's word to lead her, and that's why she thought so highly of herself. She had learned that she was GOD's specific handiwork, and that he put thought into everything about her. She knew that she was special and great in her own unique way. So when she started the list, she wanted it to help Terrance to know that he was special and great too. She gave him a good, long but sneaky look because she couldn't let him know she had his name, then she thought to herself "Number 1, he has beautiful brown skin." She looked him over a little more and said "He dresses nice," as she admired his polo hooded jacket and nice, crisp, khaki pants. She went on to say that he had a nice smile, a seemingly calm personality, and other things like that. She knew that everyone would know who she was talking about, and she hoped that they would join in on the fun and that the activity would make him feel special and loved, just like the rest of the class felt. Wendy smiled as she wrote her list. She knew in her heart that it would make Terrance smile too.

Mrs. Jordan decided to allow five people to present their lists, and the class would try to figure out which classmate it applied to. Five students would get a chance to do it at the end of the day for the entire week, so they would have something to look forward to after the hard work was done in the mornings. So, when the time came for the lists to be read, everybody was excited and wanted to be first.

Mrs. Jordan called Lisa first because everybody knew that she was the class writer, and she made all of her presentations fun. Lisa was always the best speaker in the class, too, because she was so dramatic and "theatrical," as her teachers called her. She had read Maya Angelou's poem "And Still I Rise" in the black history program last year, and she got a standing ovation. Everybody in the class looked up to Lisa, and she knew it. She didn't take it for granted, though. She took on the responsibilities of being an admired leader in stride, and she always tried to do things to make her classmates somewhat proud of her. Everybody thought that Lisa would probably be president or something important like that when she grew up.

When she started naming the traits on her list, we instantly knew who it was. "He's funny," she said very whimsically, "Loves video games, his best friend is Tommy," that was when everybody chimed in. All of the boys in our class were funny and loved video games, but everybody knew that Tommy and Corey were best friends.

After Lisa, she called Corey, Anthony, and Ciara. When she finally reached the 5th student, she said "Wendy, it's your turn."

There were only 20 minutes left in the school day, so Wendy knew she had to be quick. They had to have time to get their things together and hear announcements, so she scurried to the front of the classroom and stood firmly behind the podium, and said.

"My person is a boy." "He has nice brown skin, and he's wearing a blue polo jacket and khaki pants." Immediately, people started looking at Terrance, and he started sinking down in his seat. Wendy didn't notice because she was so focused on her list, so she just kept talking. "He seems quiet but kind, has nice brown, oval eyes, and deep dimples." He's new to the school and he doesn't seem to have friends yet because he doesn't talk when everybody else is talking, but I would love to be his friend." And with that, Wendy walked toward Terrance and held out her hand.

Everyone was looking at Terrance with smiles on their faces, but, instead of him smiling back, tears were streaming down his face and onto his cheeks like a river, and they entered the corner of his mouth, across his lips, and down his chin and neck. Before Wendy knew it, he had grabbed his books and run past her like a jet. The minute he ran out, the announcements came on, and it was time for students to start gathering their things to go home.

Wendy stood in astonishment and embarrassment as she wondered what she had done that was so wrong. No one, not even Mrs. Jordan knew what to think about Terrance's response. She ran toward Wendy and put her arms around her.

"It was so sweet of you to want to make him feel welcomed," she whispered to Wendy as she led the students in getting their things while letting the office know that he had left the classroom.

Wendy's spirit was crushed. She stood in one space and wondered how she could have messed things up so badly. "GOD, I know I heard you," she thought to herself. I asked you about everything that I put on that list, and I felt in my heart that you told me yes to each thing." she said. "So why did he act that way, LORD" she questioned GOD with persistence. "My heart was sincere, and he hurt my feelings."

The PPG gathered around Wendy and tried to make her feel better. "Don't you worry about this," Alexis said to her, "everything you said was nice." Paula hugged her and said "It sure was, Wendy, please don't feel bad."

Shrimp stood behind everybody with his fist balled up. "Yeah, I don't know what's wrong with that dude, but I plan to find out," he said while slamming his fists into his hand. No one paid him any attention because they were used to Shrimp making threats that he never made good on. He just loved to feel like he was tough.

Wendy listened to what her friends said, and she tried to feel better, but she just couldn't get past what Terrance had done. She sat down at her desk with shock on her face as she waited for her mom to come to the classroom to pick her up.

CHAPTER 6

The Evening of sweet sentiments

Wendy sat in the car in silence as she, Walter, and her mom rode home. Lisa put her hand on Wendy's leg and said, "Listen, baby," you did what you thought was right, your heart was in the right place, and that's really what matters most".

Wendy listened to her mom, but she wasn't really hearing her. Instead, she was pondering in her mind what she had done wrong, and why he had responded the way that he did. "I really tried, mama," she said. I saw him sitting by himself, and I didn't want him to feel left out, and that's the only reason why I did it." she said, sounding heartbroken.

Lisa took one look at her daughter and wished that she could take the disappointment away. It was amazing how things could change so quickly. This morning, Wendy had been on top of the world. Now, the look of sadness on her face made Lisa want to cry. She knew that there would be times when her children would be hurt, but, to be honest, that realization didn't make things better when the disappointments came.

Walter, who had been wearing headphones and playing his game, realized that Wendy was upset. He took off his headphones, sat up straight in his booster seat, and asked her "What's wrong sister, why are you so sad?"

At that moment, Wendy felt that she needed to stop wallowing in self-pity. "I'm ok, Munchkin," she said to her brother as she stuck her head in the backseat and kissed him.

Walter was always trying to make Wendy happy, and she loved him for it. She didn't want him to see her sad, so she decided to enjoy her time with her family.

The evening activities went along as usual. Wendy went to soccer practice and hit a goalie, then she came home, took a shower, and ate her favorite meal with her family. She loved chicken tenders, mashed potatoes, broccoli with cheese, rolls, and sweet tea for dinner.

When everything was settled, and Lisa had read her a Bible story (yes, she still wanted bedtime stories in 4th grade), she mentioned Terrance again.

"Baby, I know that Terrance's response to your kindness startled you."

Wendy nodded her head yes as she listened to her mom.

"You have to remember, sweetie, that your life is not everybody else's life." Wendy looked puzzled, so Lisa continued "You don't know what types of things Terrance has had to live with," Lisa said while Wendy listened intently and allowed what she was saying to really sink in. She never thought about what Terrance's home life was like. She knew she didn't know him, but her life had been so safe and secure, and she felt like that was the case with all of her classmates. Lisa was really making Wendy think when she continued talking. "Please don't feel bad for trying to help someone, my Angel, she said, GOD knows your heart, and he honors your kind desires."

When she said that, Wendy sat up in her bed and hugged her mom. Lisa always knew the right things to say, and she really needed those words right now, because she truly dreaded the thought of facing Terrance the next day.

After they embraced, Lisa got up and kissed Wendy on the forehead. Now I want you to rest well, my Angel because you still have a 4th grade to conquer. she said with the power in her voice that Wendy had come to know and love. After she said that, she tapped Wendy on the shoulder, turned on her glow lamp, and left the room. Wendy lay in her bed with a smile on her face because her mother's comforting words made her feel so much better.

CHAPTER 7

GOD, you've got some explaining to do

Wendy fell asleep for about three hours, but around 12:00 am, she woke up. She tossed and turned in her bed trying to go back to sleep, but she just couldn't seem to find any peace. Although she had just declared that morning that "Jesus Loves Me," was a baby song, she found herself requesting that Alexa play it to help her sleep. As she listened to the sweet sound of the words, she couldn't believe it, but tears were streaming down her face.

"I'm confused, GOD," Wendy said out loud. "My heart believes that you told me to say the things that I said to Terrance. I prayed about each thing. I didn't just write any old thing. I tried to create a list that came from my heart. I thought that I would be the hero in the class. Why was that opportunity taken away from me, GOD? Why was I the bad guy instead of the good guy?"

Wendy continued to toss and turn. She'd face the wall, and her mind just traveled back to that moment. She'd face the other wall and get caught up in the memory of the stares of her friends who were just as puzzled as she was when it happened, and didn't know what to say. She sat straight up in bed and decided she needed greater backup.

Wendy was given a cell phone for emergencies, but she was not supposed to use it after 9:00 p.m. Most of the time, she honored that rule, but this time, she needed help. She quickly went to her contacts and called her best friend Alexis.

Alexis's curfew was at 9:00 also, but these two knew that there were times when they just had to talk, and this was one of those times.

Alexis whispered "Hey girl, what's up?

Wendy said "Lexi, I just can't sleep," why do you think Terrance acted like that?"

"I don't know, but it sure was weird," Lexi said. "I felt so sorry for you."

"Yeah," Wendy responded, "I was so embarrassed. "Everybody was looking at me, but I was just trying to help."

"Girl, I know," Lexi said, "Just stop worrying about it." "You didn't do anything wrong, so get some sleep."

"But I can't, Lexi. I just feel so bad."

Lexi paused on the phone for a minute, then she said,

"Do you remember what we did when I thought my parents were getting a divorce?"

Wendy instantly remembered.

"Yeah girl, I know we pray about things we want GOD to do, but we never pray about him making us feel better about what has already happened."

Lexi paused, then she said, "But didn't you say that we can go to GOD for anything?"

Wendy thought about it, then said "yes, that's what my mom said."

"OK, Lexi said, so let's tell GOD that you didn't mean to make Terrence feel bad." Let him know that you were trying to do a good thing and ask him to help you feel better."

Wendy thought about it, and she thanked GOD for having Lexi as a best friend. They pressed facetime so they could see each other, then they got down on their knees beside their beds and prayed.

"GOD," Wendy said, I don't know why Terrance acted the way he did, but I do know that I was trying to be a friend."

Lexi chimed in and said, "She really was GOD."

Wendy continued. "Whatever is wrong with Terrance, please help him feel better, GOD." Please let him know that everybody in Mrs. Jordan's class wants to be his friend, so he doesn't have to break down and cry or sit alone anymore."

"That's right GOD, help him see it, please," Lexi said.

Wendy brought it to a conclusion by saying "I know that you know everything and that you can fix everything, and I pray that you will, in JESUS name, amen."

"Amen," Lexi said, as they both lifted their heads.

"Thank you girl," Wendy said, as she and Lexi rose to their feet.

"Hey, that's what besties are for," Lexi said, as they blew each other kisses and hung up the phone.

After they hung up, Wendy told Alexa to play "It's the GOD in Me" by Mary Mary as she drifted off to sleep.

CHAPTER 8

The Following Day

Wendy was nervous about stepping into the classroom the next day. Although her prayer with Lexi had given her peace last night, she woke up the next morning with her stomach all in knots again. Her mom could tell that she was nervous. She put her hand on her knee and gave her a reassuring smile in the car, then she hugged her again and told her to have a nice day before they separated that morning.

Wendy gave her mother and Walter a quick hug in response, then she made her way to the classroom. She was full of nerves because the only thing she could think about was facing Terrance, and she just wasn't ready for that. As she entered the classroom, she noticed that he wasn't there yet.

"Good," she thought to herself as she breathed a sigh of relief and tried to enjoy the day.

As the students did their schoolwork and started to prepare themselves for art class, Terrance walked into the classroom with three adults, two very pretty ladies, and a handsome, well-dressed man. Principal Adams was with all of them, and she asked to speak to Mrs. Jordan.

"Keep working on the different types of sentences, students," she said as she stepped outside. While they talked, Wendy let her mind wander to some scary places. "I'll bet they are telling Mrs. Jordan to keep Terrance away from me." she thought to herself as the jitters started to resurface." So many bad thoughts came to mind until she saw Mrs. Jordan and the other adults walk back into the room. They were all smiling, and one of the pretty ladies who came in with Terrance smiled directly at Wendy. That made her feel a little bit better.

"Have a seat, sweetheart," she said with love in her voice, as Terrance walked with his head down. He glanced at Wendy, then quickly glanced away when she tried to meet his gaze.

Later that day in their free time again, Alexis said "PPG come to order." We have to discuss yesterday's situation"

Wendy was sitting quietly. She was the President and usually presided over the meetings, but today, she just didn't have the energy, so Alexis, vice-president, took over.

"So yesterday, Alexis said, Wendy attempted a good deed.' Now my sister did her best to make someone feel loved. It didn't go over the way we wanted, but her heart was definitely in the right place. Can we all agree with that?"

All club members raised their hands and said yes.

"Don't feel bad about it Wendy girl, Paula said. The things you said were beautiful and sweet, and if that dude couldn't see it, then it's his problem."

Wendy couldn't help but laugh. Paula was the most outspoken one in the group, and she always said what was on her mind.

The other club members started to chime in.

"Wendy, you have such a kind heart," Asia said. She was an off and on member of the group, but she was nice and always supportive. "Please don't let this make you feel bad."

"Yeah," Lexi chimed in, "You're the nicest one out of all of us. We know you were trying to make him happy."

Wendy looked around and smiled at her crew. She had to remember to thank GOD for giving her such good friends.

"Thank you, buddies," she said, as she spread her arms out to invite a group hug. They all embraced and giggled and made each other fall when they saw Mrs. Jordan come to the door, indicating that it was time to go inside.

CHAPTER 9

Terrance explains

When they got back inside the classroom, Terrance was standing behind the podium. "What's going on here?" Wendy thought nervously as they made their way to their seats. They were so shocked to see Terrance standing there, and he looked like he was ready to make a speech, which was surprising because he seemed too nervous to ever say anything in front of people.

"Everyone have a seat, please." Mrs. Jordan said. We were very curious about what was going on, so we sat down quietly and waited for further instructions.

Mrs. Jordan stood beside Terrance and said "This is our new student, Terrance. I have not had a chance to formally introduce any of the students who are new to our school, but I think that Terrance made quite an impression on all of you yesterday, so I want us to get to know him a little bit better."

After she said that, she moved away from Terrance and sat behind her desk.

Terrance stood nervously, then he said "Hello, my name is Terrance." I am 10 years old, and I have moved to Indiana from Georgia for family reasons."

"Georgia," Wendy thought curiously. "That's odd. What a coincidence that we came from the same place." Knowing this made her pay even closer attention to what he said. Everyone else in the class did the same thing, but not because he was from Georgia. Even fourth graders could be nosy, and they all wanted to know what exactly those "Family reasons" were.

Terrance kept talking. "When I lived in Georgia, my home life was happy. I have a little brother named James, and my dad was a truck driver. Wendy immediately realized that he said "was," so she assumed that his parents got divorced. She tuned in more carefully as Terrance continued to talk. My mom didn't work, so she was home every day after school, and when it was like this, things were AWESOME!" Everyone was smiling in the room as he said "I would love coming home to delicious meals, fun music playing in the house while my parents danced and sang together, and my mom would shower my brother and I with warm hugs while my dad taught us how to be men. Those were some fun times. I had my friends, and life was great."

Terrance had everyone on the edge of their seats as he shared his story. The things that he said didn't sound so foreign because the life that he described was how all of them lived, but they knew that something tragic was brewing on the horizon.

"One day, I came home from school, and I just knew that things were different. "Here we go," Wendy thought, now he'll tell us his daddy left, she said to herself and she listened with her ears wide open. Terrance continued by saying "There were no fun sounds from the T.V. or radio in the house, and no wonderful smells coming from the kitchen, and my heart just knew that something was dreadfully wrong." Everybody was hanging onto every word he said. "When I walked into the living room, I saw my mom crying, and my youngest aunt was holding her. That was the moment that I found out that my dad had been killed in a trucking accident in downtown Atlanta, and that is the moment that my whole world changed." Every student in the class sighed in horror. Their hearts went out to Terrance, and some of them even began to cry, and so did he. Through a broken voice, he said, "My parents and my little brother mean everything to me. My mom was warm and loving, but my dad was tough and strong and yes, very loving too. He taught me how to shoot a basketball, how to wear my tie, and he was our Boy Scout troop leader. How could I live in this world without my dad? This couldn't be real, it just couldn't." Terrance said, and now he was sobbing. Mrs. Jordan walked up to him and embraced him. He paused for a moment, cleared his throat, and gained his composure. Soon he was ready to speak again.

Terrance continued by saying "I knew that my dad would expect me to be the man of the family, so I started consoling my mom and my brother. I couldn't let them see me cry. I'm a man, and men don't cry."

Wendy thought about her dad, and she knew that men do cry, but she continued to sit quietly and allowed him to finish talking.

Everyone in the class just listened. Nobody said anything, so Terrence just kept talking.

"Mommy didn't work and daddy had no life insurance, so we had to move in with relatives who reminded us every day that we were in the way, and they talked badly about us behind our backs." Wendy shook her head in disbelief. She couldn't believe that the family behaved this way.

"No one wanted to watch my little 3 year old brother while my mom searched for a job, and she couldn't afford daycare. It seemed like we could only get help if we were considered homeless, so we lived in a shelter for 3 days. The shelter found us housing in a neighborhood that was very scary, and around this time, my mom started drinking to help her cope with life. We were getting food stamps, but she hardly ever cooked, so my brother and I ate frozen pizzas, hot-dogs, and candy bars a lot of days."

Everyone sat in shock as they listened to Terrance's story. He would pause for a minute to catch his breath, then he'd start again. "Finally, my mother's oldest sister came down to check on us, and now things are better. She took one look at my mom and said, "You're getting help, and you're coming to live with us." She and her husband helped us get packed up, and they would not allow her to say no to their help. We've been living with them since July 10th. The people you guys saw this morning are my aunt, uncle, and mom. My mom is in recovery and she's looking for a job, and my aunt and uncle are taking very good care of us."

By this time, every student and Mrs. Jordan was crying. Everyone's heart went out to Terrance, and they all wanted to help make his move to Indiana, be a great one.

"You have a beautiful family," Mrs. Jordan said in the background. Her voice was quivering, so it was obvious that she was crying too.

"Thank you," Terrance said as he turned around to look at her, then faced the class again, specifically Wendy.

"So when you said that you wanted to be my friend yesterday," Terrance said, "I felt thankful."

Wendy felt a new set of tears begin to escape her eyes now. It was confirmed. She had heard GOD right. She didn't mess up. When she thought about what she needed to write on that list, she sat quietly and asked GOD what to say, she also sought his answers clearly and concisely, and she had heard him correctly. Wendy was so happy she wanted to scream. She sat up straight and erect in her seat, and allowed Terrance's words to fully soak in.

He continued by saying "It's been a while since I've had a chance to hang out with real friends. It's amazing how people change when they think you're not on their level anymore."

Terrance expected his classmates to look at him with pity or judgment. He did not know how to interpret their teary reactions when the whole class sat quietly in their seats and just looked at him with what he thought was pity and disgust. Finally, Wendy got up the nerve to walk toward Terrance and say, "Hi, I'm Wendy, and I would love to be your friend."

After she did this, everyone else followed. Before they knew it, Terrance was surrounded by classmates, boys, and girls, who embraced him and let him know that he was a part of a new family and an awesome set of friends.

Mrs. Jordan stood and admired the level of maturity and love her 4th grade babies had for each other. "This is definitely a good group," she thought to herself, as they laughed and talked and got to know each other better.

CHAPTER 10

A different ride home

Wendy was talking at literally 100 miles a minute on her way home in the car that afternoon. Lisa smiled and thought to herself "What a difference a day makes." Walter could tell that things were great with his sister, so he put his headphones on and played his game just to get some peace and quiet.

"Oh mama, you should have seen it," Wendy said, as she detailed the events of what happened in the classroom with Terrance that day. "There was so much love. It was awesome seeing everybody respect each other and open our arms with compassion." Nobody said anything mean or out of the way. We just embraced Terrance and let him know that he's part of us now. Isn't that great, mama? I knew GOD told me to say those things, I just knew it."

Lisa loved to see her baby be so excited. I'm happy for you my love" she said. "When you truly listen to GOD and try to do what you think he wants you to do, you won't regret it. Things don't always work out the way that we think they should. GOD is mysterious, and our ways are not his ways, but if we really try hard to please him, and we mean it with all of our hearts, he honors our desires. You're only 9 years old, but as you get older, my words will make more sense."

Wendy knew that her mom was right once again. Nothing had ever happened in her life where her mom's wisdom didn't help her make it through.

When Wendy and Walter went to soccer practice that evening, she and Alexis had a ball talking about what had happened at school that day. Alexis's mom even came up to talk to Wendy and tell her that she was so glad that things had worked out. Wendy was surprised that Alexis's dad was not there. He was their usual soccer coach, but he had been missing lately. She was happy to see her mom, though. All of the kind words made Wendy smile, and she became even more devoted to listening to GOD's voice.

After soccer practice, they ate a delicious dinner of lamb chops, rice, kale, lemonade, and strawberry tarts for dessert. After dinner and a shower, Lisa came into Wendy's room to read her another BIBLE bedtime story.

"I'm so happy that GOD showed up and showed out for you baby, Lisa said, my heart was really hurting for you yesterday."

"I am too, mommy," Wendy answered. "I know what you said is true. Everything will not always turn out the way that I want it to, but I'm sure glad this one did. I couldn't handle the guilt of causing someone else to cry."

Lisa looked at her daughter as she beamed with admiration. She was thankful to have a child who cared so much about other people's feelings.

"Thank you, LORD." she mouthed to herself as she embraced her daughter and gave her a good night peck before she turned on her lamp and walked out of her bedroom to allow her to dream sweet dreams.

CHAPTER 11

The Saga Continues

Wendy couldn't believe what she was hearing. Her cell phone was ringing, and it was 11:05 p.m. It wasn't as late as her call was to Alexis last night, but it was much later than the times when they would usually sneak on the phone.

"Hello," she said groggily. Wendy was really tired because she didn't get much sleep the night before.

"Wendy, it's an emergency," she heard Alexis say on the other end of the line, "We need the PPG in effect immediately, "Something terrible has happened.

Wendy thought to herself "Here we go again." as she listened to the panic in her friend's voice and wondered how GOD would fix it this time.

"I can't believe it, I just can't believe it" Alexis wailed as she expressed her grief to her best friend.

Wendy listened intently as she silently prayed to GOD for the best way to handle this problem. She knew she had to be there for her friend, so she put on her strongest listening ears and got prepared for the challenge

Make Predictions:

What do you think is wrong with Alexis?

Stay tuned for the next segment of Wonderfully Made Wendy and the Powerhouse Prayer

Group:

About Author

Keicia Lyons is a high school language arts special education teacher who works at Salem High School in Conyers, Georgia. She is the mother of two children (Ariana & Marquis), the nana to five grandchildren, and the only child to the late William Barnhill Jr. and Mrs. Barbara Barnhill.

Keicia's life choices and challenges are the tools that make her a kind and compassionate spirit. She is adored by her high school students because she always greets them with a warm smile and her southern maternal charm.

Mrs. Lyons has written a play titled "A Dance with Darkness," which was performed at the historic Douglass Theatre in downtown Macon, Georgia in 2003. She also wrote a children's book titled "Bridgette's Big Day in 1st Grade," in 2010. Her most recent projects include an autobiographical self-help journal titled "I'm Wonderfully Made, Are You Sure?" as well as an inspirational YouTube channel and Blog titled "Inspiration Speaks."

Keicia is very excited about what lies ahead for Wonderfully Made Wendy and her "PPG," Stay tuned for great adventures with GOD at the forefront as Wendy and her gang knock down obstacle after obstacle when they put their prayers into action.

www.ingramcontent.com/pod-product-compliance
Lightning Source LLC
Chambersburg PA
CBHW050913120626
46552CB00004B/1552